MY GRANDMOTHER'S NECKLACE

Enjoy the journey

Pat Carly

MY GRANDMOTHER'S NECKLACE

PATRICIA BRODERICK CARLEY

My Grandmother's Necklace is a work of fiction.
Names, characters, places and incidents are the products of the author's imagination or are used fictitiously. Any resemblance to actual events, locales, or persons, living or dead, is entirely coincidental.

To order additional copies of this title, contact your favorite local bookstore or visit www.tbmbooks.com

Cover and book design by Anne Smith, The Troy Book Makers

Printed in the United States of America

The Troy Book Makers
www.thetroybookmakers.com

ISBN: 978-1-935535-402

DEDICATION

I wish to honor the women of the Vik/Takacs lineage: my aunts and cousins, both living and passed away, in America and Eastern Europe. I especially give homage to my grandmother Mary, mother Margaret and sister Nancy. We embody a proud and courageous heritage.

PROLOGUE

She caresses the precious diamonds yet again. They lay flat against her white throat. A beautifully-fashioned necklace. Platinum and gems. Fire and Ice.

What a journey they made to be here today. They crossed the Atlantic Ocean so long ago, May 1912, as individual stones hidden in the secret pocket of a handmade skirt. Who knew what perils awaited young Mary in America?

Tonight, June 2009, they travel the Atlantic Ocean again. Heading East this time. First class, not Third. Adorning Mary's lovely granddaughter, Marie, as she journeys back across the endless stretch of water. This is the moment for which she came up on deck. She unclasps the strand and looks at the gems in her white-gloved hand. Are they truly real? Why were they lying there, exposed, in Grandma Mary's jewelry case? Hiding in plain sight? Like so much of Grandma's life. Hidden in plain sight.

She raises her arm to toss the necklace overboard. The ship's Captain has just announced they are traveling over the expanse where the Titanic went down nearly a century ago. This will be the perfect gesture. An anointing of the waters. A tribute to Grandma who boarded another ship that fateful Spring.

"Wait, miss. You can't throw anything overboard here. This is a sacred place. Don't do it!"

Marie stops, mid toss, and turns her head slowly, ever so slowly. She feels the wind on her face. She shudders slightly from the cold night air. She feels a hand on her shoulder, a kiss on her cheek.

"Who's there?" Marie says aloud.

Following the sound of fading footsteps, Marie sees a mist that has mysteriously appeared near the lifeboat down the deck. The mist has a shape now. Long, flowing, hair. Hands on hips. Arms akimbo.

"Grandma?"

The ghostly shape whispers, "I know what you planned to do. Don't throw it away. Keep the necklace. It's the link to your past. Our past. To Mari."

"Grandma?"

Marie hears a whooshing sound. The mist dissolves and she is standing alone, necklace clasped 'round her neck again. When did she put it back on?

The diamonds are warm, the platinum cold. Fire and Ice.

Marie decides she needs to go back to her stateroom, have a glass of wine and collect her thoughts.

Upon entering the sitting room she spies a book, open, on the chaise.

"Where did this come from?" Marie can barely whisper.

A chilled breeze floats through the room. The door closes.

"Grandma?" Marie asks aloud.

Sitting down, pulling the red, long-fringed shawl around her bare shoulders, she begins to read the page that has been offered to her. Amazed, spellbound, Marie scans, then closely reads the previously unknown story of Grandma Mary's early life and journey to America.

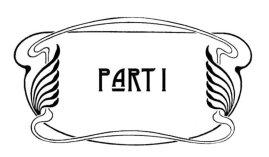

PART I

ONE

"Mary! Mary! Come here this minute! Where are you hiding, child?"

Mary stays very still, crouching low behind the scrubby tree in the back garden. She knows if she reveals herself it will bring the end to her childhood days. She has heard the talk. Her mother and father whisper in their bedroom, but Mary can hear them. She can hear whispered words two rooms away. Mary has never revealed this secret talent of hers to anyone, not even her very best friend, Veronica.

Mary knows she is being sent to some strange place, called America. Far, far away across the ocean in a big boat. She is afraid of this ocean. She is afraid of this America. Why must she go alone? She is only 16 years old. Well, not even that until the Spring. By then, she will be on a big boat with strange people going to a strange land.

Oh, please, dear Mary, mother of Jesus, don't let them send me away.

Reluctantly, Mary creeps around the side of her house and silently joins the group of adults standing in the yard. Everyone is talking at once. Some are gesturing, pointing at the sky, the ground, the Western horizon. Everyone but her own mother's mother, the old Ekaterina. Mama Kati.

Mama Kati waggles her long, gnarled fingers at Mary and leads her to one of the out-buildings in the field beyond the cluster of houses. No one seems to notice they are missing from the noisy group.

Mama Kati has Mary start digging behind a large apple tree that she has climbed up, sat in, dreamed in, watched the stars in since she was three years old. In the shallow hole Mary's hand feels something hard and square. A box! She lifts it out gently and places it into Mama Kati's hands. Mama Kati silently pries the lid off the box and whispers to Mary to take the blue velvet bag out and open it. Mary hesitates at first, knowing this moment is important to both herself and her grandmother.

Peering inside, Mary almost drops the bag in surprise. It is filled with sparkling stones. They are different sizes and different shapes, all shiny despite having been buried in dirt for who knows how long?

"Mama Kati. What are these?" Mary breathes.

"Ah, my precious child. These gems, called diamonds, were given to me by my grandmother. They, in turn, had been handed down from grandmother to granddaughter back and back and back to the time of Ogodei Khan, the son of Genghis Khan. One of Ogodei's many slave women was an ancestor of mine...and yours.... She stole these jewels from under the very nose of his favorite wife while she slept. A brave young woman, your ancestor Mari. She hid these stones so cleverly in the folds of her scant clothing, no one detected them. She slipped away from the Khan's tent one night, taking her girl-child with her, never to return, never to be found.

"You are named for her, my child. Mary Magdalene. Beloved of Christ Jesus. Beloved of me.

"You will take these diamonds and sew them into a secret fold of the new skirt we have made for your journey. You will go across the ocean to America. Like Mari, you will travel West and finds your heart's desire.

"Now, go child, and talk with your Mama and Papa and find out what you need to do to prepare for this great adventure."

"No, Mama Kati. I don't want to leave you. I will never see you again!" Mary cries.

"It is so," says Mama Kati. "We will not see one another again in this life, but we will be together with all the healing women of our family in the afterlife."

Mary runs to the circle of family members still in her yard and says to her parents that she must prepare her new clothing for the journey. She then goes into the little farmhouse and climbs the ladder to her room under the roof. She looks around at her meager furniture, her one doll Mama Kati made her long ago, her few pieces of clothing and sighs.

How will I survive alone? I am afraid of the water, afraid of the dark, afraid of lightning. Afraid, afraid, afraid....

What did Mama Kati mean, 'healing women?' Who is she talking about? Me?

Then Mary thinks about her great-grandmother back and back and back who was a slave to Ogodei Khan. And of that woman's daughter. This could explain some things that have puzzled Mary. She has always wondered why she does not look like others in her village. Like Veronica. Mary's eyes are slanted, her cheekbones high, her chin pointed, skin slightly darkened. Her family does not own a mirror, but Mary has seen her face in the water in the nearby stream and in shiny metal spoons. Sometimes the other villagers stare at her when they think she is not looking. She hears their whisperings two streets away. This is her secret, hearing the whisperings of others.

Mary's slave-girl ancestor was 14 when she fled the tent village with her baby daughter in that faraway time. Surely Mary can face her own uncertain future alone, no crying baby to conceal. Mary is leaving home because she has been 'chosen' by her family as the 'best prospect' for a future in America. Everyone has pooled their extra coins to pay for her passage and for the chaperones from Germany who will accompany her and others on the ship.

As nightfall approaches, Mary is afraid to go to sleep. Tonight, she knows, the dreams will come. But maybe this time they will not be so frightening now that she has learned about Mari who was so brave so long ago. Maybe in the morning her dreams will make sense.

Mary checks under her pillow again to make sure the bag-ful of diamonds is safe. Then she removes the bag from its hiding place and falls asleep with it clutched tightly in her hand. She says her prayers: 'Hail Mary, Our Father and Glory Be...' and falls into a deep sleep. And dreams.

TWO

She is running. Running for her very life. Clutching the baby tightly to her breast, smothering the frantic cries. She has slipped under the brightly colored tent with help from her only friend, Yoonhi. Friendships have not come easily in the world of Ogodei Khan and his huge entourage. He has swept across Asia and Europe at a ferocious pace, killing nearly everyone in his path. His men were given free rein to rape, kill and plunder whatever they coveted. Mari was coveted by many, but kept by the Khan himself. This became both a blessing and a curse for the lovely 12-year-old, known as Mari in the common language of her people. She was quick to realize her life depended upon her ability to adapt to this new life in the Khan's camp. As a consequence of Ogodei's attention Mari became pregnant and now has a one-year-old daughter to worry over and to love. She knows they must leave to live.

Mari sobs as she runs away from the only friend she has ever had and out into the unknown. If she is captured she will be tortured, returned to camp and does not want to think about what will happen after that. She must focus on living now for her daughter's future freedom.

Mary feels all these emotions in the dream state and awakens herself with a scream dying on her lips. Mary's heart pounds and her blood races through her veins. She is sobbing and the collar of her nightgown is drenched with tears. But this time when the dream is broken, Mary at least knows whom she is dreaming about. It is her namesake, Mari Magdala, the revered one. The one who escaped from the Great Khan's camp and began a lineage that encompassed two cultures, two races, one bloodline of Wise Women.

Before coming fully out of the dream, Mary remembers feeling the weight of the bag of diamonds tied at Mari's waist, under her many veils.

The diamonds! These are the same jewels she has right now in her hands. They are centuries old. Priceless. From a foreign land. They were given to her for safekeeping along with the legacy of Mari and her child.

It is sunrise now and Mary must prepare for her own journey overland to meet the German couple who will be her chaperones on the voyage. She has carefully sewn a secret pocket into the folds of her traveling skirt to hide the bag of diamonds. Even her mother knows nothing of their existence, so Mama Kati has told her. Mary does not like keeping anything secret from her mother, but she knows she must this time.

Everyone is crying while trying to be brave. In turn, Mary says goodbye to her brothers and little sister, her father and mother, Mama Kati and finally her best friend, Veronica. Her little sister is inconsolable. She does not understand why Mary has to leave. Her brothers are openly jealous.

"Why were we not chosen to go? Why must we stay behind to work the fields? Mary will be living soon in America where the streets are paved with gold and no one has to work ever again. Money is everywhere. There is plenty of food. Life is one great feast."

They turn away from her. Her father is grave and only wishes her 'Godspeed." He knows life will not be easy in America, but does not want to worry Mary and his wife with stories he has heard from those who returned, penniless. He touches Mary's cheek and goes with his sons to work in the fields.

Mary's mother is brave. She knows Mary is a skilled seamstress already at 15. She knows Mary will find work in the city beyond the sea. She also knows this is truly goodbye. It will take them many years to collect enough money to send another family member to America. Mary will most likely never come home again. She stares intently at Mary, memorizing every feature, committing to memory her voice and gestures.

Now Mary turns to Mama Kati. Kati squeezes Mary's hand, touches the bag of diamonds she knows is hidden in the skirt and whispers in Mary's ear.

"We will not meet again in this life, but I will wait for you on the other side of the veil. The day you arrive, Mary

Magdalene, will be a day of great rejoicing in Heaven. Remember me."

"I will never forget you, Mama Kati. Never."

Kati has a final parting gift.

"Take this plant with you, It is a 'magic onion' that will help you help those who are sick or injured along your journey. Be sure to keep at least one little piece of it to grow in your new home in America. It is the last offspring of the plant your ancestor, Mari Magdala, brought out of Asia so long ago. It has the power to heal, but only in the hands of a true healer. I believe you have this gift. Use it wisely and it will serve you all the days of your long life."

Mary waves and waves goodbye as the cart she rides in moves slowly down the path. The horse is old and the path is full of rocks and tree roots. This part of the journey will be rough. She must not cry and beg to stay in Hungary. This would only bring more misery to her family.

As the cart rounds the curve at the end of her small village, Mary cannot help but smile. She is excited about the adventure that awaits her. Apprehensive, yes, but also excited. How little she knows of what hardships await her. For now, her adventurous soul takes flight. She imagines she is Mari, escaping from the Khan's camp and fancies herself the bravest of the brave in her flight to freedom. To America!

THREE

A strip of blue appears in the distance. *Can this be the ocean?* Mary does not know, really, what an ocean is. She has heard the word and knows it is a vast amount of water. *But, what does it look like?*

Mary's horse-drawn cart soon crests a small hill and the strip of blue becomes a wide expanse of water. She can see the other side, barely, and thinks how easy a journey this voyage to America will be.

"Why, it is just over there. America."

When she says these thoughts out loud the man driving the cart laughs and laughs.

"Oh, my dear, this is the Danube River, not an ocean. We are still many days from the Atlantic."

The houses are set closer together now and Mary sees a church and small shops, not like home where there are just little houses with dirt floors and farms and orchards. Mary likes the looks of this village by the river and wishes she could stay, but after a short stop to refresh themselves and the horse, they travel on.

They cross the Danube by way of a wooden bridge. It is near dark now and they decide to spend the night at an inn on the other side.

Mary is so excited. She has never slept alone nor in another person's house. She falls asleep right after supper.

Heart pounding. Horses' hooves pounding. Men shouting. Mari and her baby are hiding in a clump of trees just beyond the tent village. Why did she wear a red shawl? She pulls it off only to reveal her red hair, but Mari trusts her hair will blend in better with leaves on these small trees. She wraps the scarf around her baby to keep her still. If the soldiers hear any noise that is out of place on the night air she will be discovered. She crouches lower to the ground and stills her breathing, puts the baby to her breast. She has covered her footprints by brushing over them with a branch, but these are clever men. They know how to spot a change in the landscape.

The two horsemen move on. Mari weeps with relief. She has to remain calm and think about her next move. She has to remember what the land looked like as they arrived in this village one year ago. When the stars come out she will be able to tell which way to run.

Mary tosses and turns in her sleep. She moans and cries out once. She sits up in bed and cannot recognize her surroundings. She is afraid. All her old fears come back in a rush. The dark. Strange creaking sounds. Horses neighing. Her dream of Mari is so real, she thinks it is happening right now. She can feel Mari's fear, smell the horses and sweat of the warriors, hear their curses when they cannot find her. Mary reaches for the bag in the folds of her skirt and is reassured that the diamonds are still there. She has worn her skirt to bed, afraid to take the bag out and risk dropping the precious contents.

Mary decides to pray and this calms her enough for sleep to overtake her once again. *Hail Mary...Our Father....Glory Be....*

A rooster crows. The sun is coming up over the sill of her window. Mary is awakened by the intense beams of light. Since she is already dressed, she grabs her few belongings and steps lightly down the stairs.

Mary is hungry. She did not eat much last evening because of all the emotional turmoil of the day. She was so sad to be leaving her family and friend, Veronica while at the same time excited to be going to America. Also, she was anxious about the journey ahead. She thinks about her dreams of Mari and knows her own journey should be less frightening. Mary is being sent by her family to a new, wonderful life full of possibilities, while Mari was running for her life from enslavement towards an unknown future. Each is unaware of what lies ahead, but both are full of hope that life will be better when they arrive at their destinations.

After breakfast John is ready with the horse and cart and they take off for the next part of their overland journey. They will meet the German couple who will be escorting many young people to America...for a price.

FOUR

Marie closes the little book, puts her head back to stretch her stiff neck and rubs her eyes to ease the strain. The book is written in such a faint, tiny script. Every line is filled with words right to the margins. The English is understandable, but Marie needs to concentrate very hard to read every word.

Who wrote this story? Her grandmother or someone to whom she told her story? How did this book get into her sitting room? In these days of fear and terrorism, no one is allowed on board without a ticket. Plus, she is traveling alone and knows no one here. Who came into her room undetected? Who left this book? A mystery.....

Another mystery is how Marie became the owner of this necklace. She was unable to attend her grandmother's funeral and was not present when the estate was divided up. When she finally arrived at the house, Marie was told to take whatever she wanted from the bedroom. There, in the jewelry box Marie had always loved to look through, were her grandmother's engagement ring and this necklace. *Why hadn't the other relatives taken them? Surely her mother or aunts would have wanted these heirlooms?* But no, they were waiting for Marie.

She also took the red, long-fringed shawl that always draped the piano in the sunroom. *Could this be the same shawl Mari wore the night she fled the camp of the great Khan? How*

*could this shawl still be so beautiful and bright after centuries of use
and cleanings?*

Yet, here it is, draped now around Marie's shoulders, both
silky-warm and comforting, and satiny-cool and calming. Fire
and Ice.

Thinking over these puzzling events and the tale in the
little book, Marie dozes off and dreams, or is it a vision?

Marie reaches out her right hand and grasps the small,
outstretched fingers of another being. She does not see this
other person rather, she senses her feminine presence. Despite
the small fingers Marie believes the other one is a young woman, not a child. The name *Mari* leaps into her consciousness.
Their hands are touching across time and space. *How can this
be? Is this other hand real?*

The small hand opens and reveals a medium-sized gem.
It is deep blue and sparkling in the moonlight that comes
streaming through the porthole in Marie's room. Mari's gift
astounds Marie and she awakens to her own gasp. Looking
down, Marie sees nothing in her hand, but feels sensations of
both hot and cold. Fire and Ice.

Was this a dream or a waking vision? Either way, Marie has
connected with her ancestor, Mari, and now knows there is
another jewel out there somewhere waiting to be discovered.
Waiting to be brought back home to the owner of the diamond necklace. Home to Marie.

Now that she is wide awake Marie opens the little book again and continues to read.

Mary's journey by horse and cart continues into the next day. Since they are traveling in early Springtime there is plenty of sunlight to cover many miles each day. Mary is restless sitting in the open cart all day. She takes out her needle and some brightly colored threads and begins to embroider a pattern she created herself onto a plain piece of muslin. Mary is happiest with a needle and thread. The repetitive movements soothe her and she can daydream about her new life in America.

She knows she will not have to work there, so she is thinking of things to do with all her future free time. First, she will walk everywhere in New York City and eat ice cream from a street vendor. Next, she will look in the windows of the fancy stores and pretend she can try on the hats and scarves and dresses displayed there. She has heard of these wonders from people who went to America and wrote letters to her father's friends. She dreams of owning a red shawl.

As Mary's thoughts drift and sway with the rhythm of the cart, a red flash at the corner of her eye snaps her head up. A small, young woman carrying a baby is running, running across the field next to the cart path. A bright red shawl with long fringe at the edges slips off the woman's head and reveals auburn hair streaming behind her. She is barefoot and wearing what appear to be only veils. She carries a small baby in her arms and this little one cries out with every step taken. The young woman keeps looking behind her with frightened eyes. Mary hears hoof beats, but sees no horses. She hears the cries of men, but sees no one.

"Help me!" A whisper in Mary's ear. "Save my baby!" A terrified plea.

It all dissipates as quickly as it had arrived, unbidden, into Mary's consciousness. Only wisps of dust remain in the open field.

"Help me! Save me!" These words ring over and over in Marie's mind as she puts the book down. Marie has also heard the thundering hooves. Tasted the fear in her own mouth. *What is happening to me?*

She pulls the red, long-fringed shawl closer around her shoulders and wonders if this is the same shawl her grandmother had seen slipping from the shoulders of the young Mari. Separated by centuries, Mari is somehow able to reach out to Mary and Marie in her hour of greatest need. *How can I help her now? What will I find when I journey back to my ancestral home? Will the ghosts of both Grandma Mary and Mari await me there?*

F!VE

Mary's journey takes her into Austria where she meets her German chaperones. They are a middle-aged man and woman, pleasant-looking enough, who speak a strange, guttural language. They use gestures to make themselves understood and Mary nods and smiles and wonders what in the world is expected of her now. Other people arrive, young like herself, twelve in all. They, too, nod and smile at one another. Hardly anyone can speak to another. Mary's fingers find the bag of diamonds in her pocket and she is comforted by them. She has coins and a little paper money to give the Germans to pay for her passage. She has to trust they take from her only what they agreed upon and leave her with enough money to get through customs on Ellis Island. When she arrives in New York City, she can just scoop up some gold from the street and buy anything she desires.

They all stay at an inn the night before boarding a train that will take Mary and her new companions across the continent to Calais, France. There they will take a ferry across the English Channel to the dock where the ocean liner and her future await her.

Mary's room at the inn which she shares with three girls has a mirror on the wall. She has only seen her face in water or metal before and is surprised at the clarity of this image. When Mary takes a peek at herself, she gasps.

"My hair is red! Where did this red, long-fringed head shawl come from? My face is so thin!"

As quickly as this image appeared, it disappears and Mary sees her own dull, brown hair and round , cheerful face staring back at her. She gently touches her face and hair.

"Mari," she whispers. "Is that you? Are you hiding inside of me? Do you want to tell me something?"

The other girls, all Austrian, look at her curiously. They wonder why Mary is talking to the glass on the wall.

Mary keeps turning her head this way and that, trying to coax Mari back out. This time, to herself, she says, *Please, Mari, come to me in my dreams tonight. I will welcome you this time. I am afraid of this journey ahead of me by train and boat. Give me your bravery.*

There is a whispered response in her ear. "Yes, my many times great- granddaughter, I am always with you. You are the chosen one for this generation. You will find your brave self, hidden in plain sight. You must carry the jewels to safety over the sea."

Mary glances quickly around to see if anyone is watching, then lightly kisses her image in the mirror, knowing she is kissing Mari, too.

So many thoughts. Her mind in turmoil as she lies down, Mary, amazingly, falls immediately into a deep sleep. And dreams.

S!X

A century away Marie closes her eyes, wraps the red shawl around her more tightly and drifts off to sleep as the little book falls gently to the floor.

A dream comes at once to both Mary and Marie, but instead of dreaming about Mari and the baby, Mama Kati comes to them both with a warning.

"Mary, Mary Magdalene. My sweet grandchild. I see a terrible disaster awaiting you and your companions. Your train will take you across many mountains and plains. Then you will come to a narrow stretch of water where you will ride a small boat to a place called England. Another train ride will take you to a strange place called Liver Pool where a great ship towers high above you. I cannot see any further into the future, but I can say you will feel both

Fire and Ice.

"Remember, Mary, I am always with you and will never leave your side through all these trials."

Mama Kati fades away and her words fade with her.

"Do not be afraid....Do not be afraid....Do not be afraid..."

Marie sits bolt upright on the chaise in her sitting room. *What was that dream all about? What terrible disaster is awaiting Grandma Mary? She lived in New York her whole adult life so got there somehow. I wonder what happened? I never heard this part of the story from her. More secrets?*

Mary sits bolt upright in her little bed at the inn and hits her head on the low ceiling beam.

"Ow, ow, ow," she cries, rubbing the sore spot on the top of her head.

"Sh-h-h-h!" the other girls hiss in unison. They murmur to one another in their own language and Mary can tell they are angry with her for waking them up. Finally, their grumblings settle down and Mary thinks about the words Mama Kati has spoken to her in the dream. Even though Mama Kati has told her to not be afraid, she is. Very afraid. What disaster is waiting for her in this place called England? What is a Liver Pool? What will be the Fire and Ice she is warning her about? Mary tosses and turns and waits for the dawn.

As soon as the sun rises, the girls are roused from their beds. They are served bread with honey and coffee with lots of sweet milk for their breakfast. Then they wait outside on the platform for the train to arrive at the station.

Mary has never seen a train before and is once again excited, forgetting Mama Kati's warning of future disaster. She sees black smoke on the horizon and soon can hear the piercing whistle of the train. *Why is the whistle so loud when clearly everyone can see the train is coming? What a strange place this is.*

The train slows as it pulls into the station and the four girls who have shared a room, four others from Poland and four boys from four different countries climb into the passenger car. There is no one for them to wave goodbye to. No one's family could afford to travel this far just to say "Goodbye and Godspeed" one more time. Everyone is sad. A few of the girls start to cry. Mary comforts them, patting their thin shoulders and wiping tears from their eyes. In her own language, Mary sings to them and this calms everyone. Mary has just realized the first of her many gifts. She is a comfort to people in distress. She can remain outwardly calm in the midst of despair. She will be tested in this way many times before her journey ends.

The train picks up speed as it leaves the small station behind in a cloud of black smoke. Mary loves to watch the trees and cows whizzing past. As the train approaches a small village, really just a few huts huddled together by the tracks, Mary has a vivid vision that startles her.

Running, running, her legs pumping fast, the young red-haired girl is keeping pace with Mary's train. She holds a baby swaddled in a red, long-fringed shawl trying to cradle and comfort the little one as she runs and runs and runs. Mary realizes this is Mari. *How did she appear here, in Austria, next to this train?* Mary can hear the horses' hoof beats as they pursue Mari. She can smell the sweat of the horsemen, feel the pounding of Mari's heart, taste her fear.

In a trance, Mary walks to the open door of the train car and stands there, transfixed by the sights, sounds and smells that have enveloped her. Suddenly, Mari catches up to Mary and tosses the bundle up to her.

"Take her. Take my baby. Save her. These men will kill her, put her on a spear, take her body back to the Khan's camp as a prize. Take her, please!"

To Mary's astonishment, she catches the red bundle. She shakes her head to clear her thoughts, looks down at her arms and sees not a baby, but the red, long-fringed shawl, empty, waving in the wind. Mary looks out the doorway to see where Mari is now, but sees and hears nothing. Mari has vanished into thin air, leaving only a faint smell of roses and the fading sound of hoof beats on the air.

This vision is different from the others. This time something real has happened. The red shawl has been passed to her from Mari's lifetime to this one.

Mary quickly puts the shawl into her carpetbag that holds her few possessions and sits back down. She leans her hot forehead against the cool windowpane and tries to sleep.

Across time and space, on the Atlantic Ocean, aboard her ship bound for Liverpool, England, Marie goes out on deck. She looks up at the stars. There are so many in the deep, dark-blue void. A meteor streaks across the sky and Marie makes a wish as her Grandma Mary taught her to do as a little girl. She wishes she will find answers to her questions when she travels to Eastern Europe. She wants to find her Grandma Mary's hometown and maybe find a long lost relative. There has been no communication for many years from relatives who have been Hungarian, Austrian or Romanian depending upon the whims of conquerors after the many wars that swept through Europe over the centuries. Marie also has a new wish now. She wishes to trace her ancestry back to the time of Ogodei Khan and find the roots that took hold back then and wound their way to her. She wishes to learn all her family's secrets. Will her wishes come true?

It is too cold to stay out on deck in the North Atlantic, even this time of year. Marie pulls the shawl tightly around her slim shoulders and turns to walk back to her suite. In another two days she will disembark on English soil and begin her journey back in time.

SEVEN

As Mary's train travels across the endless flatlands of France to Calais on the Eastern side of the English Channel, she tries to learn some English words from her fellow passengers. There are so many languages being spoken here and she loves the various sounds and nuances of English, French, German, Polish and her native Hungarian. In many ways they are similar amidst their differences. Her English words include 'cow, train, ship, America, friend.'

Always, Mary's thoughts turn to America. Everything in her life depends upon reaching this golden land. She must learn to live alone and trust herself and her own instincts. She must learn to not be afraid.

"Cow, train, ship, America, friend." Mary repeats these words and points to the young girl with two pigtails perfect and straight when she says "friend." Her new friend, Hannah, will sail with Mary to New York City, City of Gold, America where they will be best friends forever.

Finally, the train ends its trip to Calais. There they will board a ferry that will transport the group across the Channel to England. They will take another train to the strange place called Liver Pool and wait for a big ship to sail them over the sea. To America!

On the ferry boat Mary starts to feel sick to her stomach. The rolling and swaying motions she loved about the train ride are now making her ill on the boat. The horizon goes up and down, opposite of the boat rail and Mary is suddenly sick over this railing. Hannah takes her below deck, lays her on a wooden bench and holds her head and hand as Mary moans and cries and prays to the Blessed Mother.

Luckily, the ferry ride is not too long and with Hannah's help Mary manages to get off the boat and onto the waiting train. The German chaperones do not want any of their young charges to be sick so they ignore her. They bustle everyone together on the train and get themselves something to eat. With everyone's extra money almost gone, the young émigrés decide to skip lunch and keep their meager savings for the long sea voyage ahead. Mary is too ill to care about lunch. She is struggling to sit upright in her seat and not look sick.

In a few hours they arrive at the dock called Liver Pool. Mary's head is aching and her eyes itch. She no longer cares what Liver Pool means nor even where in the world she is. She just wants to get on the big ship and lie down.

As the chaperones stand to one side, the young people get in a line to be examined by the ship's doctor. He makes sure they are not carrying some terrible disease to the New World. No sick people allowed in America.

Mary is now afraid. She feels so ill and must hide this from the doctor.

"Next in line!" yells the man dressed in white.

Mary is standing with Hannah, but must go alone into the doctor's office.

Please, Blessed Mother. Please, Mama Kati. Help me get onto this big ship to America. I must not be sick. I must be strong enough to leave with Hannah and the others. I cannot be left behind.

However, after the doctor looks down Mary's throat and into her eyes and ears, he declares her unfit to board the ship and says she must stay here.

"What?" Mary cries. "I go America."

This is all the English she can think of. Besides, her throat hurts too much to say any more in any language. The German couple shake their heads and turn away from her. They keep the money Mary gave them for her passage and leave her alone and ill on the dock. Hannah keeps looking over her shoulder and crying as she is pulled along with the rest of the group. As they walk up the lower gangway of the huge ship, Mary slowly sinks to the wooden planks of the dock. She wraps her newest possession, the red, long-fringed shawl, tightly around her shoulders and sobs and sobs.

What will I do now? is all she can think over and over. Her fingers find the bag of diamonds and grasp it for security.

The ship's horn blasts three times. The towering smokestacks send out huge plumes of steam. The ship slowly leaves the dock as men scurry around throwing ropes, yelling, swearing, throwing more ropes.

The crowd on the dock waves and cries and shouts their goodbyes. The people on the many tiers of decks wave and cry and shout their goodbyes.

Mary glances up from the miserable heap of carpetbag, red shawl and confetti she is lying in and, as the ocean liner clears the dock, she sees the letters that look ten feet tall on the back of the ship.

Mary's eyes are hot and her body is cold. Fire and Ice. She wonders what these letters spell....

T*I*T*A*N*I*C

PART II

E!GHT

Marie is startled awake by the sound of swishing fabric: satin or taffeta. Someone is walking past her open stateroom door.

"Who's there?" She says aloud. Then, to herself, *Why is my door open?*

"Who's out there?"

Marie remembers she had been reading the little book and now searches for it on the chaise and floor around her. *Where is it?* Looking up she sees a wisp of grayish-white mist retreating out her door and around the bend of the deck.

Marie gets up, pulls the shawl tighter around her shoulders and peers out the door.

"Hello. Is anyone out here?" Marie ventures, in a small voice. Then, bravely, Marie steps through her doorway and follows the mist down the deck. It stretches to the lifeboats securely tethered above the railing on her side of the ship. Marie chose this stateroom because of the proximity to the lifeboats. She saw the movie, "Titanic," and was not going to be left behind if this ship suffered a similar disaster.

As she slips along the steel deck Marie's eye is caught by the crescent moon with brilliant Venus hanging just below like a jewel suspended from a curved, silver choker. Like a diamond hanging from a chain. Like her Grandma Mary's diamond necklace she is now wearing. Like the way the sky looked the night Grandma Mary's ship left Liverpool bound for the open sea.

Marie gasps and feels for the necklace at her throat. In the next instant she remembers her dream, or was it a vision, of Grandma Mary's abandonment on the dock as her ship sets sail without her.

The Titanic. My God! Grandma Mary was supposed to be on the Titanic! What miracle saved her from certain death? Grandma never said she was supposed to be a passenger on the Titanic. Another secret she had kept. But why? Why not tell us how she escaped one of the greatest tragedies of modern times? These thoughts swirl around in Marie's mind just as the mist is now swirling around her knees. She feels herself being propelled towards the lifeboats ahead.

Marie feels something in her gloved hand and finds the diamond necklace there. *When did I take this off?*

As she advances towards the prow of the Queen Mary she now can see lights on the horizon. They will be docking in Ireland tomorrow, then on to Liverpool, England.

Marie realizes her Grandma Mary's story starts there, where the lights are winking in the dark night. She must follow the trail of these diamonds, if indeed they are real diamonds. Maybe that is where she will begin. At a jeweler's shop.

*Or should I just throw them overboard as I tried the oth-*er evening and be done with this strange tale?

"Marie. Marie. Follow our trail. Unwind our story. Come to us. To Mari and Mary and all the others in between. Bring the gems and red shawl. Come."

N!NE

Mary is lying in a heap on the dock at Liverpool, England as the Titanic steams away. *How could the German couple leave me here? I cannot speak this language! I cannot ask for help.* Burning with fever and wracked with chills, Mary tries to stand up. People who have been waving goodbye to the ship are milling around her. The women pull their skirts aside and whisper behind white-gloved hands. The men step around her and stride away without a backwards glance.

Mary realizes she must look crazy lying on the dock, sobbing, shaking , speaking her foreign words. *Will no one help me?*

She now can neither go back to her home nor get to America without money and a sponsor for the ship and entry at the place called Ellis the Island.

Mary's throat is raw from crying and the fever and her sobs become weaker and weaker.

Out of the crowd, miraculously, a delicate hand reaches down and touches Mary's burning forehead. It feels so cool and dry. Cold tears leak out from Mary's swollen, hot eyes. Fire and Ice.

To let this kind lady know she appreciates the gesture, Mary croaks the only English words she remembers. "Ship, America, friend." The lady smiles and strokes Mary's forehead again and pushes her sweaty hair away from her face. She says words in several different languages to see if Mary reacts to any of them. German, French, Danish, Polish. Mary sadly shakes her head no. She has come to realize these past few days on the road that her native Hungarian is like no other language in Europe. None of her familiar words are like any she has heard from her companions.

Undaunted, the kind lady smiles and motions to the man standing nearby. He walks over and after discussing something with the lady, picks Mary up in his strong arms like she were made of fine, spun wool. He carries her to a waiting carriage and gently places her on the seat. Mary is unable and unwilling to resist. She decides she must trust these people. What other choice does she have? No one else even looked at her and some even stepped on her feet as they hurried to their own carriages.

She is covered up with a blanket and, as the horse picks his way among the crowds on the dock, Mary is lulled by the swaying coach and amazingly, instead of feeling frightened, is feeling drowsy. As she starts to drift away, Mary closes her hand around the bag of diamonds and pulls the red, long-fringed shawl tighter around her shoulders. They are her only possessions now along with her 'magic onion' and few belongings in her carpet bag.

In the distance, the Titanic's horn blasts its farewell to England. The tugboats have left her side and she travels, 'full steam ahead' to Ireland. Studying her rescuer from under heavy eyelids, Mary sees she is wiping tears from her eyes with a beautifully embroidered handkerchief.

Mary wonders, *Why is she crying? Maybe she has just said goodbye to a young girl and this has led her to feel compassion for my sickness and sorrow at being left behind.* This is a game Mary likes to play. Making up stories in her head about other people's lives. As she mulls over the possible reasons this lady is being kind to her, she finally falls into a deep, fevered sleep. And she dreams.

The girl is crying, huddled behind a large rock. It is cold and dark. She no longer has the red, long-fringed shawl to cover herself. She is only wearing the flimsy veils she ran away in. She is barefoot now, too. The slippers she was wearing when she escaped became more hindrance than help. But now blisters are starting on her delicate, pampered feet. She should have been preparing for this flight better by walking barefoot when she could to toughen her feet. She should have starved herself, instead of filling up on the honeyed wine and fresh bread she loved so much. Being a favorite of the cook and wine master made her life more tolerable in the Khan's camp, but ill-prepared her for these days of flight and stealth.

Mari had brought no food nor drink with her. She just took her chance at escape when it presented itself. She has been on the run now for several days. Mari has lost track of time. Her baby is too weak now to even cry and has stopped nursing. How long can they survive like this?

Just two days ago Mari was running and running alongside a strange beast that breathed smoke. It ran in a straight line and made loud, piercing noises. Her body in pain, her breath coming in wrenching gasps, Mari looked at the side of the beast and saw, to her utter amazement, a young woman. Mari had yelled to her, 'Take her. Take my baby. Save her. The men will kill her, put her on a spear, take her body back to the Khan as a prize. Take her, please....'

The young woman leaned down toward Mari, holding her arms out to catch the baby. A miracle! Her baby will be saved! Mari summoned every ounce of courage within her being and tossed the baby bundled in the red shawl up and up to the arms waiting for her.

But, when Mari looked down at her own arms, the baby was still there and the red, long-fringed shawl was gone and the smoking beast had vanished.

"What just happened?" Mari wonders aloud to her baby. "This seems like a dream, but if the shawl is gone it cannot be a dream. The beast and woman were real. But where did they come from and where did they go?"

Remembering this, Mari feels dizzy and heads towards a little cluster of shrubs and short trees to sit in the shade and think about what to do next.

TEN

Mary startles awake from her sick, fevered stupor while a century in the future, Marie blinks rapidly and tries to shake the vision she has just experienced from her own fevered brain. As she leans against the ship's railing, Marie realizes she is feeling faint and queasy. *Why is this 'seasickness' happening now when the sea-going part of my journey is nearing an end?* She hasn't felt ill the entire voyage, just disconnected from people and events around her on the ship. She has taken this time away from her world in New York City to think and read and plan her future. Maybe she will stay in Europe for an extended time. There is nothing and no one dear enough to keep her in America right now. She feels strongly that Eastern Europe will be her new residence. The spirits of her ancestral grandmothers are pulling her ever Eastward. Home.

Meanwhile, Mary is shivering and crying in the beautiful bed her lady rescuer has put her in. A girl, close to Mary's age, has taken Mary's clothing from her and washed her dirty, tired body and half-carried her to the bed. The bed and room it is in are so magnificent Mary can hardly believe her eyes. Soup, warm bread and hot tea are brought in on a silver tray the likes of which Mary can only dream about owning. She is allowed to eat sitting up in bed. *Eating in bed. Will wonders never cease?* As Mary is somewhat revived by the hot soup and tea she notices what a lovely dressing gown she is wearing. It has lace at the collar and cuffs. She could make something like this herself. She is daydreaming about lace and pillows and hot tea when suddenly Mary remembers her own dirty, ragged clothes she was wearing.

"Oh, no!" Mary cries aloud.

To herself she agonizes, *Where is my skirt? Did they throw it away or worse, burn it up? Where are the diamonds Mama Kati gave me? Are they lost too? Thrown away or stolen by the servant girl? Oh, dear God, help me! And what of my red shawl? Oh, this too much to bear!*

Hearing Mary's cries, the kind lady rushes into the bedroom. Unable to understand why Mary is sobbing and thrashing about, the lady tries her best to hold and comfort her. As she calms down, Mary realizes she will have to use gestures and her few English words to ask for her personal treasures.

"America, friend, ship....Oh! Oh!" Mary wails.

She points frantically to her chest and shoulders, pantomiming wrapping herself in the shawl. The she pats her thighs and runs her hand along one leg hoping she looks like she is putting her hand into a skirt pocket. Mary repeats this over and over and suddenly the kind lady's face lights up.

"Oh, my dear child, you are worried about your clothing. I had everything washed and hung outside to dry. Your beautiful red shawl is safe." She pantomimes wrapping herself in a shawl while nodding and smiling to show Mary she has kept this item safe. The lady has a puzzled look as she rubs her hand along her thigh. But, again, a smile lights up her face and she jumps up from the side of the bed and walks quickly down the stairs. When she returns it is with the red shawl and a small, blue bag tied tightly at the top with a string.

She smiles as she hands these things to Mary and Mary grabs them and holds them tightly to her chest smiling and smiling.

Shyly, Mary leans over and kisses the kind lady on the cheek and points to herself and says, "Mary. Mary Magdalene."

"Well, Mary, Mary Magdalene, I am Sophia. Sophia Byrne. Pleased to make your acquaintance."

"So...fee...ya. Please too," stammers Mary in return.

They both smile and hug one another.

ELEVEN

As the Queen Mary docks in Liverpool on May 12, 2009, Marie wraps the red, long-fringed shawl around her shoulders, touches the diamond necklace at her throat and picks up her tapestry valise. She waits by the ship's railing and watches the First-class passengers leave the ship by way of the long gangway. These men and women carry nothing themselves except a small dog or jewelry case. Even their children are led by frowning nannies who seem unimpressed with being in England. Marie supposes the servants' lives are the same, endlessly boring days no matter where they are. There are limousines lined up at the dock and even one horse-drawn carriage waiting for some wealthy couple wanting a romantic entrance to the British Isles.

Marie likes to watch people and make up stories about them in her head. She fantasizes about their lives and loves and hopes and dreams. Marie feels a little hopeless right now. She knows she is attempting to run away from her life in New York City. Here she is sailing to Europe to forget her past while her Grandma Mary was sailing the opposite way full of hopes and dreams towards a bright, new future. And, what of that small, young girl with the baby who keeps invading Marie's dreams? She is always running and running .

All of us are on the run to and from somewhere. Will we ever arrive at our destination?

Marie is determined to find and follow the trail of Grandma Mary and Mari and discover where their three lives intersect. She believes there is a place and a moment in time when they will all meet face to face and heart to heart.

This shawl and these diamonds hold the keys to everything.

It is now Marie's turn, from Second-class, to descend the gangway and step foot on British soil. *Is this the same dock where Grandma Mary fell into a fever and missed her place on the Titanic?* Whether it is or not, Marie says a prayer of thanks that her grandmother missed the ship that day and was left behind. Tonight she will read from the little book to see if she can decipher more of Grandma Mary's tale.

Marie has booked a room in what she hopes is an authentic British B&B. She hails a taxi from the dozens lining the dock and is swiftly deposited at a lovely Victorian house a few blocks away.

"At least the outside looks like the photo on the Internet," Marie says in a low voice. "If the inside is as cheerful and cozy, my first night will be a happy one."

"Here ye are, Miss," says the taxi driver and he hauls her steamer trunk up the short flight of steps to the front porch. "You can go right in."

As Marie opens the door, a soft chime rings through the entryway and a young woman appears in an apron wiping the flour from her hands and shooing a cat from the settee by the door.

"Oh, my. I heard a horn blast from the Queen M II but thought I had more time to get these biscuits in the oven. I like to offer my guests hot tea and a little something to eat before dinner, which is at 7 o'clock and is in the oven right now and there's the kettle whistling at me and oh, my, you must be tired and want to see your room and get those boots off and put your feet up. Listen to me going on and on. My name in Sophie. Sophie Maria Magdalena Powell. Whew, that's a mouthful for any girl."

When Sophie finally takes a breath, Marie replies, "I would love to go to my room and rest a bit. Thank you kindly."

They ascend the highly polished wooden staircase and enter a room decorated all in white. Marie is so pleased to see a big, comfortable bed with a chaise lounge by the window. She glimpses the sea between the trees and sighs with contentment. She will be able to get some rest here.

Sophie is prattling on about the furniture and how old everything is and who made it. When she gets to the dresser she says how the old, sepia photographs are placed about for atmosphere.

"People like to think everything in England is an antique, so when I found these old photos in the trunk in the attic, I had them framed and put around."

Marie picks one up and immediately puts her hand to the diamond necklace at her throat and gasps.

"Where did this photo come from? I have one just like it on my dresser at home. This is my Grandma Mary as a young woman. She was a maid for a wealthy family in New York City. How did you get this picture?"

"Oh, that picture. I'm named after her. She was my Great-grandma's personal maid for awhile back near the turn of the last century. Mary Magdalene, she was, from Hungary, bound for America. But she stayed here for about a year for some reason or other. I heard the story a few times over the years, but don't remember the details right now. I'm also named for my Great-grandma Sophia. Sophia Byrne. Do you know who she was?"

Marie's head is spinning and the nausea has returned.

"I..I must lie down for a bit, Sophie. I'll come downstairs to have tea a little later."

Marie lies down on top of the bed holding the photo to her chest. Tears slide down her face. She cannot believe she chose this B&B over the Internet! The very house her Grandma Mary lived in and apparently worked in for a year. She always believed Grandma Mary went straight to New York City and worked there as a maid. Grandma never spoke about being a maid here first. She never said this photo was taken in Liverpool not New York City. More mysteries surrounding her grandmother. More secrets.

Marie opens the little book and looks for confirmation of the events she has just been made aware of and yes, it is all here.

TWELVE

Mary agrees to stay on with Sophia since she truly has no where else to go. Sophia is delighted to have Mary's companionship as her husband and daughter travel abroad. She teaches Mary English and finds her to be an eager student. Mary knows if she is to make a life for herself in America she must be able to speak and understand the language.

Each day Mary gets stronger and healthier. Eating good English food puts a glow on her face and in her eyes.

April 15, 1912, five days after Mary's arrival at Sophie's house, the first telegraphic message arrives in Liverpool that the Titanic had hit an iceberg the evening before and help is on the way. No one is to worry, the Titanic was built to withstand any disaster at sea. But, as the day wears on, the messages change in tone and it is difficult to discern the facts from the speculations.

"Titanic hits an iceberg but stays afloat and all are rescued."

"Titanic is steaming on to New York City, crippled, but seaworthy."

The messages go on and on into the night. Finally, official word reaches the people of England and the news is tragic.

"Titanic strikes an iceberg 400 miles off the coast of Newfoundland. The hold quickly fills with water and within 2 1/2 hours she sinks to the bottom of the Atlantic Ocean. Only a few hundred of the 2200 passengers and crew escape in lifeboats. All the others are drowned as the Titanic breaks apart and sinks."

Sophia and Mary are glued to the wireless in the living room all day and evening and into the morning of April 16th. They realize this latest report is the true story. In all probability Mary's companions and Sophia's family are gone. Drowned. Dead. At the bottom of the sea. Mary cries and cries at the enormity of this loss of life.

Sophia is distraught with grief and guilt. She had refused to accompany her husband and daughter to America. She was afraid of the sea-crossing. She was afraid of the size of the Titanic. She was afraid she might drown. She was afraid, so stayed behind. She cannot accept that her family is gone so she and Mary walk to the telegraph office and then the newspaper office to see if there is a list of names, living and dead. The survivors of this disaster are now being posted slowly. Too slowly for waiting relatives and friends.

It takes time to interview and list all the passengers who have been plucked from their lifeboats by rescue ships. The survivors are taken to New York City. Nearly everyone waiting there is hysterical with grief and fear. Interpreters must be found for those who do not speak English. There is chaos among the waiting families on Ellis Island until all of this is sorted out.

In England, the families wait and wait for news. Mary and Sophia comfort one another as best they can. One minute they are hopeful, the next they are sure their family and friends are dead. Another night and day pass and now more names are coming in. Sophia learns her daughter is alive. Alive! But alone in America as her husband's name is among the missing. Sophia immediately has a telegram sent to her cousin in Philadelphia, urging her to go to New York City, find Philomena and stay with her until they can arrange passage back to England.

Mary thanks God and the Blessed Mother that she has been saved from certain death. She should have been on that ship! What if her parents learn of this disaster? They knew she was sailing on the Titanic. Her village is remote, but this news could make it's way there.

How can I get word to my mother that I am safe? I must write a letter. They have no telegraph office like here in the city. No post office for that matter. How will it reach them? I must at least try. Mary works this over and over in her mind. *When Sophia is calmer I will ask her to help me. Right now she needs to be taken care of.*

Exhausted, the two women fall into chairs by the wireless. The sunlight streams into the sitting room windows, but they do not care about the sun. They do not care about the lovely flowers blooming outside. They do not care about dinner. They gaze between the trees to the sea beyond. Silent, grief-stricken, they slip into uneasy sleep.

TH!RTEEN

Mary falls into a frenzied dream. She is lost in a strange land. Nothing looks familiar. Not the trees. Not the few flowers. Not even the stars overhead. She is running and running but getting nowhere. She is frightened. She looks down at her legs to see she is still running in place, but now the land has turned into water. Cold, dark water. Her running legs are treading in this water, keeping her head above the dark, freezing sea. She looks around. People are everywhere. They are screaming for help. Crying. Moaning. It is so cold, Mary can barely breathe.

"I am so cold. Blessed Mother, help me. Help all of us!"

Mary realizes she has been talking out loud, but no one is responding to her. Each person is crying out to God, to their mothers, to the moon and stars.

Mary looks down again and sees a baby in her arms. Blue. Dead. As she starts to scream everything turns black.

Mary awakens with a start and finds herself in Sophia's sitting room. Her face is wet with tears or is it seawater? She tastes salt. She quietly gets up to go splash cold water on her face and as she tiptoes across the hallway she is startled by a face at the front door. The man's hand is raised to knock, but Mary hurries to open the door before Sophia is awakened.

"Is Sophia Byrne at home? I must speak with her. Now."

Mary shrugs her shoulders to indicate she does not understand what he is saying.

"Please, may I come in?"

Mary sees he wants to come into the house, so she lets him walk past her. She points to the sitting room where Sophia is beginning to rouse herself, then backs into the hallway again.

"Yes? What is it you want, Alfred?" asks Sophia.

Ah, thinks Mary, Sophia knows this man. He looks so grave. This cannot be good news.

"Sophia, my dear. Please sit back down. Have this young lady get you a cup of tea." Alfred has a kind voice and sad eyes.

"No. I don't want a cup of tea, Alfred. Just tell me what you came to say." First, Sophia sounds angry then she ends up whispering, "No. I don't want to hear this. No...."

"Sophia. I was at the telegraph office just now and a new list of well.... They know now who all the survivors are. All the rescue ships have docked in New York City. Everyone's names have been given. I am so sorry, Sophia. Dennis' name is on no list of survivors. He is lost. Lost to you and Philomena. To us all."

"But, Alfred, just because his name is not on a survivor list does not mean he isn't still alive. He may be out there, somewhere, in the ocean. Floating. Swimming. Exhausted. Waiting to be rescued. Please, Alfred, we cannot give up hope." Sophia nearly screams these last words.

"No, Sophia. No. The water was below freezing. No one in the water was able to survive that. Those not already in the water or in the few lifeboats went down with the Titanic as she slid beneath the waves. I am so sorry, my dear. So very, very sorry."

FOURTEEN

Weeks have gone by now and Philomena has come back to England accompanied by Sophia's aunt from Philadelphia. Her homecoming is glorious, yet filled with sorrow. Philomena's daddy is not here. She had hoped he was secretly here, at home, waiting to surprise her when she came back. This hope was the only thing that could get her on a ship again. But, he is not here and her life must be filled by her grieving mother and Mary.

Mary and Sophia have become great friends over the past month. Their tragic losses have bound them together and, even though Mary is dressed like a maid, she is no servant to Sophia. Sophia has decided Mary must learn an occupation or trade of some kind and settles on training her to be a maid of the highest quality so she can get a wonderful job in New York City with a wealthy family on Fifth Avenue.

Imagine me, living on Fifth Avenue, New York City, America. The street that is paved with gold, Mary thinks to herself. She practices her English day and night and is quick to learn anything domestic. She had worked hard back home, so is not afraid of chores to be done. Sophia is teaching her to do these chores with grace. Sophia pays Mary for her work and in ten months time Mary has enough money to book passage on the ship S.S. Amerika. Can she be as brave as little Philomena and get on a ship and cross the wide ocean to a place she has never seen before and can only imagine?

Please, dear Jesus and Blessed Mary. Give me the courage to pick up my life and sail to America. Help me to not be afraid of a sinking ship and the dark water. Mary prays this each night.

Marie puts the little book down on the nightstand. Sophie calls up to Marie that it is time for dinner and since it is only the two of them this evening if Marie would like, " we could sup in the sitting room overlooking great-gran's flower garden. If you look through the trees just right you can see the ocean. I'll open the window a crack so's you can hear the sea gulls jabbering to one another. I hope you like what I cooked. It's just fresh bread, vegetable soup and hot tea. Since you were looking kind of peaked this afternoon I decided to make something hot and delicate for you delicate condition."

Marie is stunned by this last remark. "What delicate condition? I just felt a bit seasick at the end of the voyage and then dizzy when I saw my grandmother's photograph. I'm fine now."

"Pardon me saying so, Marie, but you are pregnant or my name isn't Sophie Mary Magdalena Powell, which it is, so there you are!"

Marie knows Sophie is speaking the truth. The truth she has been keeping to herself for several weeks now. The truth she kept from Charles when she decided to sail to Europe for an extended stay. The truth that, spoken aloud, might have changed her mind and made her stay in New York with Charles. Stay in an impossible relationship.

Marie had been fearing for her own sanity. The dreams and visions and voices whispering in her ear and crowding into her thoughts at all times of the day and night. She decided she was going insane and needed to get away from everything and everyone. She needed time to sort all of this out. She loved Charles and they had wanted children right from the start of their marriage. But, as the years slipped by and no child appeared, Marie began to think there was something wrong with her. She had been afraid to find out so never consulted a doctor, even though she told Charles she had. Oh, the deception of it all! She couldn't bear it one more day, so she concocted the story of tracing her family's lineage from America back to the old country. Marie thought this trip would answer some questions about the family. Charles agreed a sea voyage would be 'just the ticket' to getting Marie 'back on track' again. *Really, Charles had a saying for every situation,* Marie thought. *How annoying. To Charles life is black and white. I am so lost in the grayness of it all and cannot take his optimism one more minute. I must get away and think this all through. Alone.*

Now, as Marie has finally decided to make this journey and discover whatever is hidden in her grandmother's past, this miracle has occurred.

"Yes, Sophie, you are quite right. I am pregnant. About three months along. No one knows back home and I want to keep it that way for the time being. Thank you for the lovely supper. I do feel better. I think I will read a little before turning in for the night."

"Goodnight, Marie. Don't you worry a bit. The angels are with you, I can see them all around you. Sleep well."

F!FTEEN

Marie goes back to her room on the top floor, under the eaves. She feels like she has been here before. Maybe this is the room Grandma Mary slept in when she lived here with Sophia. *Did Sophie tell me that earlier? I can't remember.*

I am so distracted lately I don't know what was said to me or what I have dreamed up.

Before opening the little book, Marie wraps the red, long-fringed shawl around her shoulders, puts on the diamond necklace and lies back on the chaise. Instead of reading, Marie immediately slips into a dream or is it a vision? No matter. The face of a darling little girl appears in her mind's eye.

Huge, hazel eyes. Almond-shaped and exotic looking. Her eyebrows are dark and well-defined for one so young. Her hair is black and straight as an arrow. Such a sharp contrast to the pale skin, small nose and rosebud lips. This child is a perfect blending of the Chinese hordes who swept into Eastern Europe so long ago and ravaged the fair, rosy-faced natives living in the land for generations, untouched by the outside world.

This child is Mari's baby. The one who has been kept hidden until now, always covered by a red shawl. *Why can I see her face now? If this is a dream how can I be asking questions about it? Is this real? A time-travel of some sort?*

The little girl holds her hand out. She is slowly opening her small fist which has been holding fast to something. A light reflects off of several surfaces in the tiny hand. Marie sees small stones. No, they are gems. Yes, they are diamonds. The little girl is offering the diamonds to Marie. She is smiling and nodding her head up and down, coaxing Marie to take them. In an instant, the little girl is pulled backwards and disappears, to be replaced by a gray mist that swirls and swirls until it, too, disappears with a "whoosh."

Marie sits up and blinks several times.

"Wow! What was that?" Marie feels a fluttering in her abdomen.

"Isn't this too soon to be feeling my baby kick? But, I think it just did." Marie says aloud to herself and her baby.

After taking a few sips of the now-cold tea, Marie opens the little book and is eager to learn if Grandma Mary has herself had more dreams of Mari. Their connection is growing stronger. Marie can feel it. The three women are swirling towards one another like the gray mist a moment ago. *When will we converge?*

Marie reads how Mary packs her belongings into a new carpetbag given to her by Alfred, Sophia's brother-in-law. He has been dropping by the Victorian house once a week this past year to help Sophia with Mary's education. He pretends to be the man of the house and Mary must wait upon him, light his pipe, get his tumbler of gin and call him in to dinner at the proper time. She thinks Alfred just enjoys being fussed over, but she is grateful for the practice.

Sophia thinks Mary is ready to work as a maid in a fine home or penthouse apartment in New York City. Mary still cannot imagine what a penthouse is, but it must be grand to live high off the ground, higher than the trees.

Alfred has snapped a picture of Mary in her uniform as a remembrance for Sophia. He will send a copy to Mary when she sends her new address to them in a few weeks.

Since Mary never got a reply from her parents she is sad to think they believe her to be dead at the bottom of the sea. Surely, they have heard about the disastrous voyage of the Titanic by now and grieve for the loss of her.

Mary has already sent a telegram to her Aunt Katerina in New York City that she is on her way, once again, to America. Her aunt will be waiting for her at Ellis Island.

Sophia, Philomena and Mary cry all the way to the dock in Alfred's horse-drawn carriage. Mary arrives in style this time and, after passing the doctor's inspection, is guided to the gangway for Third-class passengers. She will have a room she shares with two other young women and a bathroom down the hall. This is paradise compared to steerage. Mary feels a little guilty about this favored treatment, but is grateful for Alfred and Sophia's generosity.

Mary is wearing a new dress and has sewn the little bag of diamonds into a new secret pocket in its folds. She has wrapped the red, long-fringed shawl around her shoulders and over her head as it is a windy day. The sun is bright in the sky, but there is a bit of cold in the air for a May day.

"Good-bye! Good-bye, my dear friends," Mary cries as she reaches the deck railing. She leans way over as she waves and waves to Sophia, Philomena and Alfred. Unless they travel one day to America, this if their final farewell. This is the third time Mary waves good-bye to people she will never see again.

The S.S. Amerika pulls away from the dock and Mary runs to the back of the ship and keeps waving to her friends until she can no longer see them or the dock or the skyline of Liverpool. Everything has disappeared into the gray mist that surrounds them all.

Mary turns around and walks slowly along the deck to find her room. The shawl and diamonds give her great comfort and she prays for her safe passage to America, the land of her dreams.

Right now, I am all alone in the world. I am out to sea without a friend by my side. This is not how I had planned this voyage a year ago. Mary sighs as she strolls along.

"You are never alone, my little one. I am with you always. Remember?"

"Mama Kati. Is that you? Why haven't I heard your voice for a year? Where have you been?" Mary says aloud.

"Do not be afraid, my precious child. I have been watching you. Who do you think sent illness your way that fateful day? I have been watching and waiting. I will be with you on this voyage. Do not be afraid. You are never alone."

With that, Mama Kati's voice fades away, but Mary feels her presence as she looks ahead, out to sea. To America.

The S.S. Amerika, which originated in Germany and stopped for more passengers in England, is finally steaming out to sea. As Mary walks to the Third-class section looking for her berth and roommates, she hears all kinds of languages and accents being spoken and shouted from fore to aft. She learned these two nautical terms from Alfred but is not sure what they mean. Left to right or front to back? No matter, the passengers are fascinating for Mary to watch and listen to. There is laughter and tears, crying babies, shouting children, men with booming voices, women cooing to their little ones.

This must be how it will be in New York City with people from all corners of Europe living together, Mary muses.

When she hears a Hungarian accent, she stops and smiles at the women and shares a word or two.

Strolling on, Mary encounters sailors who whistle at her admiringly. She has never had this attention before and finds she rather likes it. When she gets to her room, she sees the other two girls have already chosen their beds and she is on the top bunk. Mary is happy about this since she can see out the little porthole and look at the stars at night and dolphins that swim alongside the ship during the day.

Mary opens her carpetbag and is very happy to discover her 'magic onion' in there. Sophia had put it in the sunny window of the sitting room and Mary had forgotten to pack it this morning. Mama Kati had given her the 'onion' her last day in Hungary and it would have been so sad to no longer have this connection with her family. Mary used the 'onion' many times over the past year. She would crack open one of the thick stems and spread the ointment over kitchen burns, Philomena's many bug bites, rashes, scrapes and even the ankle of Alfred's favorite horse when he was limping a few months back. Mary knew she would find many uses for her 'magic onion' on board ship and again in America. She is grateful Sophia remembered to put it in her bag.

Mary's roommates burst into the little room, laughing. They are round, rosy Romanian girls, looking very much alike. Sisters, acting like best friends. Mary knows she will have fun with them and suddenly misses her own sister, now eight years old, who Mary always thought of as a pest. She feels a sharp longing for this sister who thinks Mary is dead.

The days go by as the ship sails on and on, day and night, through rain showers and sun showers. The third day out, there is an announcement that they will soon be approaching the part of the Atlantic where the Titanic went down.

Mary runs to the ship's railing and looks and looks at the glass-smooth sea. It has been a year, but maybe some piece of something has floated up to the surface and is lying there waiting for Mary to see it.

Was that something shining in the water? A reflection of the sun off a piece of glass? A mirror? Or is it just my imagination running wild, as always?

Mary whispers a prayer for each of her former companions and even the guardians who took her money and left her on the dock, sick and alone. How could they know her fate would be better than theirs? They left her without a backward glance and now were most likely at the bottom of the sea.

Mary shivers, pulls the red shawl more tightly around her shoulders and puts her hand in her secret skirt pocket to hold the bag of diamonds for comfort. This time her fingers feel something more that a few small stones. She takes the bag out, opens it and with a sharp intake of breath sees that the diamonds have been fashioned into a necklace. Sophia and Alfred must have done this!

There are more gems on this strand than I had in the bag.

As she holds the necklace up to the sun, Mary sees the diamonds have been alternated on the chain with beautiful crystals. To an inexperienced eye, the gems look all the same. Mary realizes how clever Sophia has been to hide the valuable diamonds in plain sight for safe keeping. Mary intends to keep it this way and leave the necklace right out in the open so people will think it is made only of crystals.

No matter how difficult life becomes in America, Mary vows she will never sell nor trade the necklace. It will be handed down from grandmother to granddaughter as Mama Kati gave the gems to her. In this family, it will stay.

As Mary holds the necklace up, the jewels and crystals reflect the sunlight, throwing brilliant rays everywhere. It looks like it is ablaze in her hand, yet it is cold to the touch.

Fire and Ice.

S!XTEEN

Mary's heart is on fire. Her ship, the S.S. Amerika, is steaming towards New York harbor. Everyone on board has been talking about the Statue of Liberty and how magnificent this enormous, green lady is. How she stands for liberty and freedom in the New World. All the passengers from steerage are up on deck and rushing forward to get a better view. Even the passengers in First-class are at the railing. They, too, are excited to be either home again or starting out on an adventure in America.

Mary is so grateful they have made it across the Atlantic alive. She is standing between her Romanian friends. They have their arms around one another and are alternately laughing and crying with excitement.

At long last a small figure is seen in the distance.

Is it green?

Is it the great Statue of Liberty?

Yes, it is she!

People are cheering. However, there are some saying "Is that the statue? What is so exciting about this green lady with spikes on her head?"

Mary thinks these people are trying to act nonchalant about arriving in New York City. She ignores them and cheers with the rest.

The three girls run to their room to collect their meager belongings and check under the beds and in the bathroom to make sure they have left nothing behind. They do not have much and do not want to leave one little thing on the ship. They go back on deck and wait by the railing like everyone else.

Mary feels a prick of fear in her stomach and wishes she had guardians with her to explain what is happening. Because Alfred and Sophia made sure she traveled in Third-class, Mary had no need of a chaperone. She could use one now. The S.S. Amerika is steaming straight past the big, green lady, past the island with so many buildings and people waiting in lines, and on up a river past the impossibly tall buildings and streets she knows are paved with gold.

What is happening? Why are we not stopping in New York City? Where are we being taken? How will my aunt ever find me? Mary shivers with fear and looks wildly around her for the two Romanian girls. They have been separated in the crowd as people push and shove to get a better view of America. Mary grasps her carpetbag tightly, rearranges the red, long-fringed shawl, ties it in a knot across her chest to keep it from slipping off her shoulders, and clutches the bag with the diamond necklace still safely tucked into the secret pocket in her skirt.

Tugboats are alongside the S.S. Amerika now, pushing and pulling her up this river. The tall buildings and trees on the right look like they are floating lazily down the stream to the ocean behind them. Mary knows she is the one moving, but the illusion is hypnotic. Looking up at the clouds makes her feel dizzy, so she tries once more to find her friends.

Mary pushes her way through the crowd, away from the deck railing and sees the many people she shared this journey with. Some look frightened, others laugh, and still others are crying. No one seems to know what is happening.

Here is the red-faced Irishman who played the hand drum while his pretty wife and little girls danced the high-stepping jig. Here is the Polish man who played the accordion and tried to keep up with the Irishman's fast tempo. Over here, cringing against the stairway wall, Mary spies her two Romanian friends. They are frightened by the pushing crowd and they, too, wonder why the ship has not stopped to let them off.

An hour later, the S.S. Amerika is pulled into a dock past the tall buildings and in an area that looks like a lovely park. The gangplanks come down, but it is clear only those in First and Second-class will be let off. There are no planks connected to the Third-class deck and certainly none for steerage. Mary and her friends stand with their mouths gaping open as the rich are escorted down the gangways. Women in huge hats and tight-fitting, bustled silk dresses carry their little dogs while servants carry their children. The men have already disembarked to find their chauffeurs or hail cabs. Their huge steamer trunks are being off-loaded and stacked at precarious heights up and down the dock. These dazzling women look neither right nor left, but give orders to their maids with nary a glance in their direction. Maids and servants are not visible as human beings to these wealthy people.

It is clear they also do not have to go through customs or the many stations at Ellis Island to be admitted to America. Mary wishes she were rich enough to do as she pleased. But soon, she will be. The streets of New York City are paved with gold even though none of the streets here look like they are.

At the very least, Mary will live with a wealthy family. She will travel the world with them and not have to go through customs as the maids she observed did not. Attaching herself to someone rich will be advantageous. Mary is already learning the ways of the New World and she has not even landed there yet.

Miraculously, the S.S. Amerika is turned around in this narrow river by the tugboats and pulled back down towards the ocean. The whispers start among the crowd.

"Ellis Island. Ellis Island."

Mary pulls her friends to the railing on the left side of the ship now and as the tall buildings stream past them once more, she points out the big, green lady standing on an island all alone with her arm permanently up in the air. The ship slowly pulls into the dock at Ellis.

Please, dear God, let me pass this examination and move on to whatever comes next.

Mary knows she needs a coin to pay someone for allowing her to be questioned and examined. This makes no sense to Mary, but she has her coin ready in her pocket. She makes sure the Romanian girls have theirs also.

Now the steerage passengers come up to her deck and they all mingle together as the three gangplanks are put out for them to descend.

Mary slows her pace and the Romanian girls finally get tired of walking with her and race ahead to be off the ship and onto American soil.

Mary wants to savor this moment and is glad to be alone now. She walks around the deserted deck, stands by one of the lifeboats and thinks again about the Titanic. She whispers a prayer of thanks that she was not on that ship. She thanks God for her happenstance meeting with Sophia on the dock and her year with her, Philomena and Alfred in Liverpool.

Proudly wearing the red, long-fringed shawl as if it were a fancy silk outfit and clutching the diamond necklace in her skirt pocket, Mary picks up her carpetbag with the 'magic onion' inside and steps onto the gangway.

She is the very last passenger to leave the ship. She nods to the sailor who holds out his hand to steady her. She lifts her small, booted foot, leans forward, and steps lightly, but boldly, upon Ellis Island.

Mary knows she has just arrived home.

EPILOGUE

Marie puts the little book down and lies back on the chaise. She closes her eyes and folds her hands across her abdomen. Into her mind's eye comes Mari with her almond-eyed daughter, and her Grandma Mary. Through the baby girl Marie knows she is carrying the circle will be complete. Mari has been trying to reach her through dreams and visions and now will be a part of her in this baby. A window into the past was opened when Marie decided to travel to Europe and trace her family's matriarchal history. She has been guided every step of the way. How else could she have ended up staying in the very house Grandma Mary lived in a century ago? Marie will continue her journey East and unravel Mari's story. She will trace the history of the diamonds that were in the possession of Mama Kati so long ago. How did a poor, peasant woman come to own diamonds? The shawl is another mystery. It is finest silk and has remained beautiful and vibrant all these years. What is the shawl's story? And, where is the blue jewel Mari showed her?

The baby flutters again and Marie sighs and smiles.

"Go to sleep, little Marika. You have a long journey ahead of you. At the end of it we will know who we are."